A Note to Parents

For many children, learning math is [...] math!" is their first response — to whicl [...] add "Me, too!" Children often see adults comfortably reading and writing, but they rarely have such models for mathematics. And math fear can be catching!

The easy-to-read stories in this **Hello Reader! Math** series were written to give children a positive introduction to mathematics, and parents a pleasurable re-acquaintance with a subject that is important to everyone's life. **Hello Reader! Math** stories make mathematical ideas accessible, interesting, and fun for children. The activities and suggestions at the end of each book provide parents with a hands-on approach to help children develop mathematical interest and confidence.

Enjoy the mathematics!
• Give your child a chance to retell the story. The more familiar children are with the story, the more they will understand its mathematical concepts.
• Use the colorful illustrations to help children "hear and see" the math at work in the story.
• Treat the math activities as games to be played for fun. Follow your child's lead. Spend time on those activities that engage your child's interest and curiosity.
• Activities, especially ones using physical materials, help make abstract mathematical ideas concrete.

Learning is a messy process. Learning about math calls for children to become immersed in lively experiences that help them make sense of mathematical concepts and symbols.

Although learning about numbers is basic to math, other ideas, such as identifying shapes and patterns, measuring, collecting and interpreting data, reasoning logically, and thinking about chance, are also important. By reading these stories and having fun with the activities, you will help your child enthusiastically say "**Hello, math**," instead of "I hate math."

—Marilyn Burns
National Mathematics Educator
Author of *The I Hate Mathematics! Book*

To the Roman family,

especially Jesse

—J.R.

For Monica, twenty-three

years and counting.

—M.L.

ISBN 0-590-64399-1

Copyright © 1999 by Scholastic Inc.
The activities on pages 43-48 copyright © 1999 by Marilyn Burns.
All rights reserved. Published by Scholastic Inc.
SCHOLASTIC, HELLO READER!, CARTWHEEL BOOKS
and associated logos are trademarks and/or registered trademarks of Scholastic Inc.

Library of Congress Cataloging-in-Publication Data
Rocklin, Joanne.
 Just add fun! / by Joanne Rocklin; illustrated by Martin Lemelman.
  p. cm. — (Hello reader! Math. Level 4)
 Summary: Hank and Frank must count, add, and multiply to figure
out the right amount of food for their party.
 ISBN 0-590-64399-1
 [1. Arithmetic—Fiction. 2. Parties—Fiction.] I. Lemelman, Martin, ill.
II. Title. III. Series.
PZ7.R59Ju   1999
[Fic]—dc21   98-20849
                                                                CIP
                                                                AC

12 11 10 9 8 7 6 5 4 3 2 1   9/9 0/0 01 02 03 04

Printed in the U.S.A.   24
First printing, May 1999

Just Add FUN!

by Joanne Rocklin
Illustrated by Martin Lemelman
Math Activities by Marilyn Burns

Hello Reader! Math — Level 4

SCHOLASTIC INC.
New York Toronto London Auckland Sydney

Chapter One: A Nice Day For A Party

One beautiful spring morning, Hank said, "Let's have a party today."

"Is it your birthday?" asked his brother Frank.

"No," said Hank.

"It's not mine, either," said Frank.

They checked the calendar, just in case.

"Your birthday is a long way off. So is mine," said Frank. "Maybe today is a holiday," he added.

"No holidays to celebrate today, either," said Hank. He sighed. "I'd still like to have a party."

"It is a nice day for one," said Frank.

"That's it!" said Hank. "We can have a 'Nice Day for a Party' party."

"Good thinking!" said Frank.

"Let's get to work," said Hank.

Frank and Hank set up a table.
They blew up some balloons.
They put out party goodies.

"We each get two gingersnap cookies, three peppermint candies, and four gumdrops," said Hank.

"Yum!" said Frank.

They put on party hats and sat down.
"What a nice day for a party," said Frank.
"Right," said Hank. "The sun is shining."
"The sky is blue," said Frank.

"But there is something wrong with this party," said Hank.

"Really?" asked Frank. "What is wrong?"

"Let me think," said Hank.

"I know! We need some music."

Frank brought out his guitar. He sang a little song:

This is a party
For you and me,
With cookies and candy,
And bubble gum tea,
Gingersnaps two, peppermints three,
Four gumdrops each from the gumdrop tree.

Frank danced around the backyard as he sang.

"There is still something a bit wrong," said Hank.

"I know, I know," said Frank. "We don't really have bubble gum tea or a gumdrop tree."

"No, it is something else," said Hank. "There are only two of us at this party. A party needs more people."

"You're right!" said Frank. "But how many guests shall we invite?"

"How many chairs do we have?" asked Hank.

"We have six chairs," said Frank.

"One chair is for me and one chair is for you," said Hank.

"Then we can invite four more guests," said Frank.

"Good thinking," said Hank.

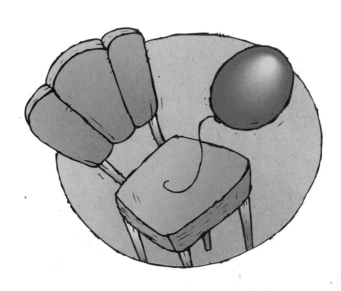

Chapter Two: The Shopping List

Frank called Sue, Todd, Mike, and Flo. "Come to our 'Nice Day for a Party' party at two o'clock!" he told each of them.

Hank found a big pad of paper and a pencil.

"We have party goodies for ourselves, but we will need some for our guests. Help me make a shopping list," he said to Frank. "Gingersnap cookies. We need two gingersnap cookies for each of our four guests."

"Two plus two plus two plus two," said Frank.

"And let's not forget the peppermints," said Hank. "Three for each guest."

"Three plus three plus three plus three," said Frank.

"And now the gumdrops," said Hank. "Four each."

"Four plus four plus four plus four," said Frank.

"Now let's see how many of each treat we need," said Hank.

"Adding everything on this list will take us a long time," Frank said.

Just then the phone rang.

"That was Todd," said Frank. "He can't come to our party. He forgot about his dentist's appointment."

"Now we have three guests, not four," said Hank. "We will have to make a new shopping list."

Hank threw away the old list.

"Let's begin again," Hank said.

"Gingersnap cookies. Two each for three guests."

"Two plus two plus two," said Frank.

"Peppermints," said Hank. "Three each for three guests."

"Three plus three plus three," said Frank. "This shopping list will take us all day!"

"Gumdrops," said Hank. "Four each for three guests."

"Four plus . . ."

The phone rang again.

"That was Sue," said Frank. "She wants to bring her two little sisters, Meg and Jenny. I told her to bring another chair."

"Good thinking," said Hank. "But now we have five guests! We have to make a new list."

Hank threw away the old shopping list.

"Gingersnaps," he said. "Two each for five guests."

"Two plus two plus two plus two plus two," said Frank.

"I know! Let's count by twos!" said Hank. "That will make things go faster."

"Good thinking!" said Frank. "Two, four, six, eight, ten. We need to buy ten gingersnaps."

"Peppermints. Three each for five guests," said Hank.

"We better hurry," Frank said. "Three plus three plus..."

Suddenly Hank stopped writing. He threw away the list.

"What are you doing?" Frank asked. "We need that list!"

"I know a faster way," Hank said.
Hank wrote on his pad.

$$5 \times 2 = 10$$
$$5 \times 3 = 15$$
$$5 \times 4 = 20$$

"See? I counted up by fives," said Hank.

"How did you do that?" said Frank.

"Look. Five times four is 5, 10, 15, 20 gumdrops. Get it?" said Hank.

"So five times three is 5, 10, 15," said Frank. "Got it!"

Hank took $10.00 from the money jar.

"Let's go shopping!" he said.

$20.00

$7.00

Chapter Three: At the Store

"Wow! Look at that!" said Frank. "We don't need our shopping list after all."

"A cake shaped like a rocket ship! What a great cake for our party," said Hank.

"Uh-oh," said Frank. "Look at the price."

"Maybe we could buy half of that cake," Hank said.

"I don't think so," said Frank. "Anyway, it is too big to carry home."

"We have enough money for this cake," said Hank.

"Put it into the cart," said Frank.

"Here are the gingersnap cookies," said Hank. "Each box has four rows. There are three cookies in each row. Let's see, if I count by threes, four times three is 3, 6, 9, 12 gingersnaps."

"No, no," said Frank. "You are holding the box the wrong way. Each box has three rows. And there are four cookies in each row. If I count by fours, three times four is 4, 8 —"

"Silly," said Hank. "We are both right. The answer is twelve both ways."

"We only need ten cookies for the party," said Frank. "We can eat the two leftovers on the way home."

"Good thinking," said Hank.

Hank put the cookies into the cart.

"Look at all that candy!" said Hank. "Yum!"

"Twenty-five gumdrops per bag," read Frank.

"We only need twenty gumdrops," said Hank. "There will be five left over."

"I know!" said Frank. "We could eat the five leftovers on the way home, too."

"I think we should share one leftover gumdrop with each of our guests," Hank said.

"You're right," said Frank. "We can give them five gumdrops each instead of four."

"Good thinking," said Hank.

And Hank put the gumdrops into the cart, too.

"Here are the peppermints," said Frank.
Frank took 15 peppermints out of the bin.
"Let's see. Our five guests will get three peppermints each," Frank said.
"Three peppermints cost 10 cents," said Hank. "Let's count by tens."

my World of
Brave Knights

Lady Megavere

'The pen is mightier than the sword'
Meg lives in an urban castle surrounded by
high roofs and flint walls. At night when
the drawbridge is up and the portcullis is
closed she feels safe and warm and writes
tales of daring adventures which she will
never experience (she hopes).

Lucy d'Ancealot

'per ardua ad astra'
Lucy, former damsel in distress,
now spends her days happily, in
courtly splendour, with her knight
in shining armour, painting
pictures of her favourite things.

We would like to dedicate this book to our knights in shining armour
Sir John, St Jonathan and *Lord Patrick of Holt.*

This edition published in 2009 by
Zero to Ten Limited
Part of the Evans Publishing Group
2A Portman Mansions
Chiltern Street
London
W1U 6NR

First published in 2003 by Zero to Ten Limited.
Copyright © 2009 Zero to Ten Limited
Text © 2003 and 2009 Meg Clibbon
Illustrations © 2003 Lucy Clibbon

British Library Cataloguing in Publication Data
A catalogue record for this book
is available from the British Library

ISBN 978 1 84089 550 6

Printed in China on chlorine-free paper
from sustainably maintained forests.

Contents

What is a knight?

Definition:

Someone who is awarded special honours
for bravery, chivalry and good deeds.

What do knights look like?

A knight can have hair which is brown, black, blonde or ginger.

A knight can have eyes which are brown, hazel, green or blue.

Some knights are tall, fair and confident.

BUT most knights
should have...

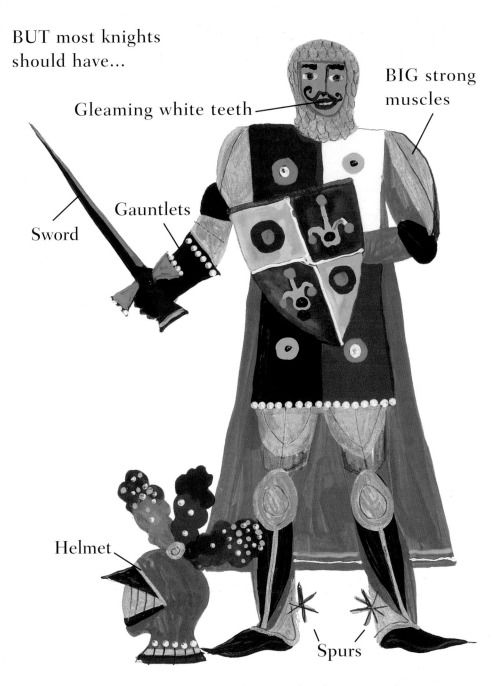

Gleaming white teeth

BIG strong
muscles

Sword

Gauntlets

Helmet

Spurs

...and must be very handsome (unless you happen
to be very ordinary looking – but very brave).

Knights in shining armour

The full panoply of battle armour was made up of many different sections. When fully dressed from head to toe, a knight could be wearing as many as twenty pieces of steel plate armour, as well as chain mail underneath, a plumed helmet, spurs, a sword, spear and shield. He was so heavy that a special sort of crane had to hoist him into the saddle and his great war horse would also be wearing armour. If he fell off, he was out of the battle because he could scarcely move.

Damsels in distress

In the days of medieval knights the world was a very dangerous place and it was believed that women (damsels) should be protected from danger. Girls were brought up to do sewing and singing and not much else. They were supposed to live safely at home in their castles, but somehow they always seemed to be getting into trouble and needed to be rescued by knights in shining armour. Nowadays, of course, girls appreciate courtesy and consideration, but they can probably protect themselves!

Becoming a knight

If you want to become a knight you have to
become the pupil of someone who is a knight
already. You have to do exactly what he tells you
for years and years and years. Not many people
can manage this, which is why there are not
many knights. You have to learn to be brave and
bold and strong. You have to practise fighting
(which is easy) and practise very polite
behaviour (which is hard).

Chivalry

This is the very important code of honour which all knights follow:

1. Protect the weak.

2. Fight wrong.

3. Be loyal to friends.

4. Seek justice.

5. Be true, gentle, faithful and brave.

6. Rescue damsels in distress.

Dare to do right!

Equipment and accessories

Ladders for climbing towers

Swords and bows and arrows

Chain mail

Carrots and sugar lumps for horse

Chocolates and flowers for damsels

Toothbrush (and teeth whitener)

Metal polish for armour

Helmet

Shields

Transportation

Knights have to do a lot of
travelling. They can either
get out and about on a *horse*
(damsels in distress love
them, but they need a lot of
grooming and looking after),
a *motorbike* (good for cities
but quite noisy), a *fast car*
(the preferred option but not good for the environment)
or a top-of-the-range *bike* (good exercise
but only useful for short journeys).

What do knights do?

Knights spend their time on quests, tasks and
thrilling adventures rescuing people in trouble.

Quests

These are long and difficult journeys which knights
make in order to find something. It is not always very
clear what it is that they are supposed to be finding.
It could be a secret treasure, a firebird, a long-lost city,
a famous sword or anything. Whatever it is, it is always hard to
find and surrounded by hidden danger. The most well-known
quest of all was to seek the mysterious Holy Grail, which was
a special chalice lost in the mists of time.

Tasks

These are almost impossible jobs or tests, which are usually set for knights by damsels in distress. An example of a task might be: find the secret drawer in the magic casket. Solve the riddle you will find there. Only then can you ask the damsel to marry you.

Adventures

There is nothing that knights enjoy more than going off on dangerous and exciting adventures. They often encounter enemies and have to outwit them or fight them with skill and bravery. After these adventures they come home to the sound of trumpets and swooning fans. They toss their armour to waiting servants and sit down to a banquet. What a life!

Dragons

There is always a downside to every job and for a knight there is a real risk of coming across a dragon. Dragons like eating knights, even the armour, so they are very dangerous. They live in mountain caves and breathe fire. Knights don't like killing dragons, but a knight may win the hand of a beautiful maiden if he slays one.

Kissing

When damsels in distress have been rescued,
they often want a kiss.
Here are step-by-step instructions:
1. Approach damsel with big smile.
2. Take damsel's hand gently but firmly.
3. Pucker lips.
4. Aim at damsel's hand.
5. Make contact.
6. Unpucker lips with
smacking noise.
7. Retreat.
8. Keep
smiling.

Knights and words

Silent letters

Have you noticed that there are silent letters in the word knight? Can you spot the silent letters in these words?

wrist fasten climb knife gnome
calf lamb wrap gnaw

Courtly language

Knights live in castles and palaces where everyone is very, very polite. They need to know courtly language. Examples:

Your wish is my command, madam.
Ever your humble servant, sire.
Many apologies if I have offended you.
Please do me the great honour of allowing me to accompany you to the pavilion.

Heraldry

When knights were all dressed up in armour it was difficult to tell who was who, and in a battle it is inconvenient to kill someone on your own side. So knights started wearing colours and badges to distinguish one from another. Pennants, shields and surcoats were emblazoned with an individual knight's colours and coat of arms. Here are some of the symbols which are part of the language of heraldry:

Chevron   Cross   Roundels   Saltire   Lozenge   Bend Sinister

The Knights of the Round Table

King Arthur and his adviser, the Wizard Merlin, gathered together all the finest lords of the kingdom and, with his great sword Excalibur, he knighted them. A hundred and fifty knights joined Arthur around the Round Table in Camelot and these brave and honourable men were sent out to fight evil. The bravest knight of all was Lancelot, but even he was not good enough to find the elusive Holy Grail.

23

Knightly things to do

Design your own coat of arms

First, draw a shield and then draw inside it
symbols of things you like, or are good at,
e.g. a football, some crossed cricket bats,
musical notes or things that say something
about you. Colour it in your favourite colours.
You can then reproduce your coat of arms and use
it to decorate your possessions
or the door of your room.

Motto

Make up your own motto.
This is a short phrase which describes what
you plan to do or achieve as a knight.

Draw a dragon

A dragon is a brilliant thing to draw, with shining
scales, pointed talons, a long tail and, of course,
fire and smoke gushing from its mouth.
Make yours as fierce and menacing as possible.

Eggscalibread

When knights return from quests
and adventures they love
to eat this simple snack.

You will need:
a large lump of butter
slice of thick bread
1 egg
4 tablespoons milk
various toppings

Directions

Beat up the milk and egg.
Soak the bread in the mixture.
Heat the butter in a pan and fry the eggy bread on
both sides until brown.
Sprinkle with cinnamon and brown sugar, jam,
or sugar and lemon or trickle on maple syrup
or other toppings of your choice.
(Ask an adult to help when heating the pan.)

Sir Boris the Bold

the story of a brave knight

*I*t's not an easy job being a knight and, when Sir Boris the Bold got back home to his castle after slaying dragons, rescuing maidens in peril and doing lots of good deeds, he was exhausted. His armour was rusty, his helmet was dusty, his socks had holes in them and his horse was fed-up.

"What I need," he said to his squire, "is a nice princess to look after me. She can bring me my breakfast in bed, mend my socks and polish my armour."

"Princesses don't do things like that," said the squire. "They aren't trained for it. They are trained to be beautiful and helpless."

"Well, alright," said Boris. "You'll just have to do the hard work and she can concentrate on being beautiful. That would work just as well. Now where can I go to find a princess?"

"You need to go to Lady Lovely's Royal Dating Agency," said the squire.

So, the next morning, Sir Boris knocked on the door of the dating agency and said that he was looking for a beautiful princess.

"Oh, and she must be very rich because the castle roof is leaking and needs to be repaired," he added.

"Well!" said Lady Lovely. "Everyone wants a beautiful rich princess these days, but I'll see what I can do. Come back tomorrow."

The next day Sir Boris arrived and found two princesses waiting for him. They were both very beautiful and had jewel-encrusted dresses and soft white hands, which showed that they were rich and helpless. The first princess, Regana, had a frosty smile and rather haughty eyes. The second princess, Dorabella, had a happy face and kind eyes. Princess Regana inspected Sir Boris the Bold's armour and Princess Dorabella admired his horse.

"Where did you get that armour?" scoffed Princess Regana "It is so last season!"

Princess Dorabella just happened to have a carrot in her designer handbag and fed it to the horse herself with her soft white hands.

"Now," said Lady Lovely. "In order to win the hand of a beautiful princess you must complete a dangerous task. You must cross the Scorpion Desert, swim the crocodile-infested river, find your way through the Goblin Forest and climb the Jagged Mountains. At the top of Peak Peril there is a magical tree. Bring back the most precious object hanging from its branches and a princess will be yours."

So, Sir Boris the Bold packed his toothbrush, his trusty sword, his swimming shorts and his climbing boots and set off on the dangerous journey. He cleverly avoided the scorpions in the desert by crossing it in the middle of the day when they were having lunch. When he got to the river he threw the crocodiles his leftover sandwiches, which kept them busy while he swam across. Going through the forest was easy because he sang at the top of his voice, and the goblins were so frightened that they all ran away. So, at last, Boris reached the Jagged Mountains and put on his climbing boots. Up he climbed, higher and higher, past eagles' nests and dragons' caves. Puffing and panting he finally reached the top and there, on Peak Peril, stood the magical tree. It shimmered and glinted in the sunshine.

Now, hanging from its branches were two objects. The first was a beautiful necklace sparkling with enormous diamonds, sapphires and rubies. The second was a birdcage with a little brown bird inside.

I wonder which is more precious, thought Boris to himself. The necklace is very valuable and any princess would love to have it. Surely that must be the most precious object hanging from the tree?

He stretched out his hand to take the necklace. At that moment he caught sight of the little brown bird looking at him. Its eyes were sparkling brighter than any diamond. Suddenly, full of doubt, Boris drew back his hand.

"Life is more precious than jewels, so I will take the little bird," he said.

Boris lifted the cage down from the tree and then set off to retrace his steps home.

"I do hope one of those wretched princesses is going to be worth it," he muttered, as he struggled heroically through the forest, river and desert.

At last he arrived back at the Royal Dating Agency expecting a hero's welcome. He was a little disappointed. Lady Lovely gave him a nice cup of tea and a doughnut and his squire gave him a wash and brush up.

"I wish I had become a footballer instead of a knight," thought Sir Boris. "They get all the fun for a lot less work."

Lady Lovely summoned the two princesses. Princess Regana arrived in a golden coach with dozens of servants. When she heard that Sir Boris had left the beautiful necklace behind she flew into a terrible tantrum. She shouted at her servants and stamped her feet.

"Go back and get it," she screamed. "Or you won't get me!"

"Good," replied Sir Boris. "I don't think I want you any more, anyway."

So Princess Regana went off in a huff.

Princess Dorabella galloped up on her favourite unicorn. When she heard that Sir Boris had chosen the little brown bird instead of the necklace, she said, "Good choice!"

"Why, thank you, Princess Dorabella," said Boris.

"Please, do call me 'Doris', all of my friends do," she replied.

"I was rather hoping we could be more than friends," Boris said. And with that he got down on one knee and asked for her hand in marriage. And, of course, she said yes – well, this is a fairytale, after all.

Sir Boris took his princess back to his castle and together they let the little bird out of its cage. Immediately it started to sing a beautiful song all about love and stuff. After they had mended the castle roof, Boris and Doris had a wonderful wedding and lived happily ever after.

my World of
Brave Knights

Knights are chivalrous, strong, handsome and, above all, brave. In *My World of Brave Knights*, you can read about the knightly adventures of Sir Boris the Bold, and discover everything you need to know about being a knight, from saving damsels in distress to slaying dragons!

Other titles in this series:

www.lucyloveheart.com

Now take more pennies, buttons, or beans so that you have 24 all together. Arrange the 24 into rows so that there is always the same number of pennies, buttons, or beans in each row. Can you arrange them in two rows? Three rows? Four? Five? Six? What size rows are possible?

Cookie Riddles

For each riddle, use your pennies, buttons, or beans to help you figure which box has more cookies.

Which has more cookies — a box with four rows and three cookies in each or a box with five rows and two cookies in each?

Which has more cookies — a box with seven rows and two cookies in each or a box with three rows and five cookies in each?

Which has more cookies — a box with six rows and two cookies in each or a box with three rows and four cookies in each?

Making Change

In Chapter Three, Hank and Frank were at the store. They found a small cake for $7.00. They also found gingersnap cookies for $2.00, gumdrops for $1.00, and peppermints that were three for 10 cents. Explain how Frank figured that buying fifteen peppermints would cost 50 cents.

Hank and Frank had $10.00 to spend. They didn't have enough money to get everything. How much more money did they need?

They decided not to buy the cake, but instead to buy the other snacks plus seven sodas for 50 cents each and a bag of peanuts for $1.00. How much change did they get from $10.00?

Cookies in Rows

You will need 12 pennies, buttons, or beans. Arrange them like the gingersnaps on pages 26–27.

Hank saw four rows with three cookies in each row. Point to the four rows Hank saw. We write this as 4 x 3 — four groups of three. We say, "Four times three." To figure how many, Hank counted by threes — 3, 6, 9, 12.

Frank saw three rows with four cookies in each row. Point to the three rows Frank saw. We write this as 3 x 4 — three groups of four. We say, "Three times four." To figure how many, Frank counted by fours — 4, 8, 12.

There is the same number of cookies either way, so Hank and Frank are both right!

Presto Change-O

Frank counted by 2's to figure out how many gingersnap cookies they needed for five guests. He counted five twos — 2, 4, 6, 8, 10. Does this make sense? Hank wrote down 5 x 2 and he counted two fives — 5, 10. Does this make sense?

Then Hank counted three fives for the peppermints — 5, 10, 15. He could also have counted five threes — 3, 6, 9, 12, 15.

For gumdrops, you could count five fours or four fives. Try it to be sure you can get the same answer of twenty either way. Count out loud.

Skip Counting

Counting by twos, threes, fours, fives, or by any number, is called skip counting. It's called skip counting because you don't count all of the numbers, but skip some each time. When you count by twos, you count every second number. When you count by threes, you count every third number. When you count by fours, you count every fourth number. A number chart can help you learn to skip count.

Skip counting with some numbers is more difficult than for others. Encourage your child to point to numbers when counting. If needed, help out by counting along with him or her.

And for gumdrops, he said, "Four plus four plus four plus four." How many gumdrops did they need?

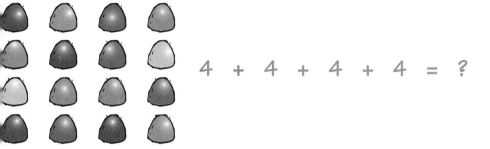

$$4 + 4 + 4 + 4 = \,?$$

Then Todd called to say he couldn't come, so Hank and Frank had to figure what they needed for only three guests. How many gingersnap cookies would they need now? How many peppermint candies? How many gumdrops?

Sue called to say she wanted to bring her two little sisters. Now there would be five guests, so Hank and Frank had to figure again! Can you figure out how many of each snack they need to buy?

Gingersnap cookies	$2 + 2 + 2 + 2 + 2 = \,?$
Peppermint candies	$3 + 3 + 3 + 3 + 3 = \,?$
Gumdrops	$4 + 4 + 4 + 4 + 4 = \,?$

How Many Snacks?

Hank and Frank decided to give each guest at their party two gingersnap cookies, three peppermint candies, and four gumdrops. In Chapter Two, they tried to figure out how many of each they needed to buy for four guests.

For gingersnap cookies, Frank said, "Two plus two plus two plus two." How many gingersnap cookies is that?

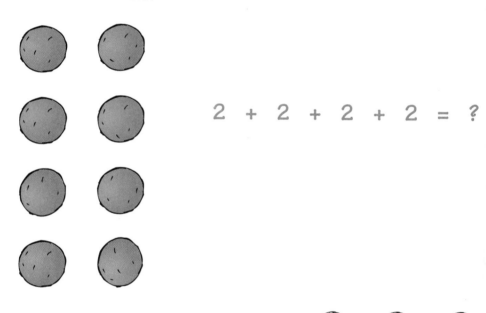

$$2 + 2 + 2 + 2 = \ ?$$

For peppermint candies, Frank said, "Three plus three plus three plus three." How many peppermint candies would that be?

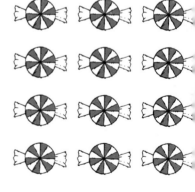

$$3 + 3 + 3 + 3 = \ ?$$

• About the Activities •

When adults think about learning multiplication in elementary school, many remember memorizing times tables. But learning about multiplication calls for much more. Children need to see when and why multiplication is useful. They need to understand how multiplication relates to the world around them. They need to learn how multiplication relates to addition and also how it connects to rectangular arrays. Learning times tables is important, but an emphasis on memorization is only appropriate after a child has a firm basis of understanding and has had a good deal of experience using multiplication to solve problems.

Just Add Fun! presents a story that helps children understand what multiplication is and helps them learn when to use this basic operation of arithmetic. The activities in this section will help you guide your child's learning. Enjoy them and have fun with math!

— Marilyn Burns

> You'll find tips and suggestions for guiding the activities whenever you see a box like this!

"Want help making your shopping list?" asked Hank. "We know where you can get a great cake."

Frank took out his guitar.

"Let's sing!" said Frank.

This is a party
For you and me,
With cookies and candy
And bubble gum tea,
Gingersnaps two, peppermints three,
Five gumdrops each from the gumdrop tree.

Then they all played hide-and-seek and computer games.

"I like this 'Rainy Day' party," said Flo. "Any day is a nice day for a party!" said Hank.

"Guess what?" said Mike. "It's my birthday next week. You are all invited."

Frank gave each guest a towel to dry off with.
Hank asked his mom to make a fire.
Then everyone ate the party goodies.

"Surprise!" Hank and Frank's mom said. "Here is a bag of marshmallows. You can roast them on the fire."

Everyone took a marshmallow.

"There are seven marshmallows left in the bag," Hank said.

"There are seven people here," Frank said.

Everyone took another marshmallow.

"Yum!" said Sue.

PLOP! PLOP! PLOPPITY-PLOP!!!

"Grab your plates and come inside!" yelled Frank.

Everyone ran into the house.

PLOP!

"Except for one thing," said Hank. "It's not a nice day anymore."

Frank looked up. The sky was not blue.

PLOP! PLOP!

"Uh-oh," said Sue.

"Its raining!" said Mike.

"And five gumdrops!" said Sue's little sister Jenny.

"And we have party hats and balloons, too," said Sue.

"Not only that," said Frank. "We each have twenty peanuts and a soda."

"There is still something very wrong with this party," said Hank. "Very wrong!"

Frank jumped up from his chair. He looked angry. "There is nothing wrong with this 'Nice Day for a Party' party!" said Frank.

Everybody put on a party hat and sat down.

"What a nice party!" said Sue.

"There is something a little bit wrong with it," said Hank.

"Wrong?" asked Mike.

"I will get my guitar," said Frank. "We need some music."

"Music is a good idea," said Hank. "But there will still be something wrong."

"What's wrong with this party?" asked Mike. "Everybody has two gingersnap cookies."

"And three peppermints," said Flo.

Chapter Four: Something Is Wrong

All the guests arrived on time.
"Welcome!" said Hank.
"Let's begin the party!" said Frank.

"Peanuts! Yeah!" said Frank.

Now the boys had enough money for everything. Hank gave the check-out person a ten-dollar bill. He put the change in his pocket. The boys left the store. Each of them had a bag.

"That cake looked good," said Hank. "But we got more for our money."

Frank bit into a gingersnap cookie.

"We sure did," he said.

"I think we should buy the cake another time," said Frank.

"I think you're right," said Hank. "This cake is better for a birthday party. Besides, I have another idea."

Hank went to put the cake back.

Frank waited on line.

Hank was back in no time. His arms were full.

"Look!" he said. "I have a soda for each guest, and one for each of us, too. And check out this bag of peanuts."

Hank checked the shopping list.
"We have everything on the list," he said.
The boys waited in line. Soon it was their turn.
"Uh-oh," said Hank. "We spent more than
$10.00! We don't have enough money!"

"Ten, twenty, thirty, forty, fifty. The peppermints will cost fifty cents," said Frank. "Good thinking," said Hank.